For Sheila Northcutt, who lived it, and for
Aria Northcutt, who will one day hear the stories —*N.G.*

Thanks to globe-trotting Mom and Daddy; you made us
citizens of the world —*E.Z.*

ACKNOWLEDGMENTS

Every book has its angels, and *Poems in the Attic* is no exception. I'm indebted to several friends for sharing their stories of growing up as military brats. Thanks to Norie Roeder, Michelle Green, Sheila Northcutt, and most especially Nancy Martineau. Where would this book be without you? The memories you shared gave my story wings.
—*N.G.*

LEE & LOW BOOKS INC., 95 Madison Avenue, New York, NY 10016, leeandlow.com
Book design by Kimi Weart
Book production by The Kids at Our House
The text is set in Raleigh Roman and Rotis Serif Italic
The illustrations are rendered in acrylic, oil, and collage
Manufactured in China by Toppan, March 2015
10 9 8 7 6 5 4 3 2 1
First Edition

Library of Congress Cataloging-in-Publication Data
Grimes, Nikki.
Poems in the attic / by Nikki Grimes ; illustrations by Elizabeth Zunon. — First edition.
pages cm
Summary: A young girl learns much about her mother as she reads a collection of poems written before she was born that capture her mother's memories of living around the world and growing up as a child of an Air Force serviceperson. Includes author's note, list of Air Force bases, and explanation of the free verse and tanka poetry forms used.
ISBN 978-1-62014-027-7 (hardcover : alk. paper)
[1. Moving, Household—Fiction. 2. Military bases—Fiction. 3. Mothers and daughters—Fiction.
4. Poetry—Fiction.] I. Zunon, Elizabeth, illustrator. II. Title.
PZ7.G88429Poe 2014   [Fic]—dc23   2014010354

POEMS IN THE ATTIC

by NIKKI GRIMES

illustrations by ELIZABETH ZUNON

LEE & LOW BOOKS INC. | NEW YORK

Poems in the Attic

Grandma's attic is stacked with secrets.
Last visit, I found poems Mama wrote
before I was born, before I was even imagined.
She started when she was seven—same age as me!

Air Force Brat

Thanks to Captain Grandpa
My mama had a childhood on wings,
flitting from place to place.

Cedar Box

I choose you to keep
all my rememberings safe,
poems about home,
no matter where that might be.
Each place is special to me.

Grandma Says

Memories can be like sandcastles
the waves wash away.
My mama glued her memories with words
so they would last forever.

Cabrillo Beach
CALIFORNIA

*Home on leave, Daddy
took me to the Grunion Run!
Our flashlights found them—
slim fish, silver as new dimes,
wiggling ashore to lay eggs.*

Bedtime

Grandma sings me to sleep
with one of Mama's poems.
I dream of skies
my mother's eyes have seen.

Aurora Borealis
ALASKA

My brother and me
held hands, breathless, as we watched
this dancing rainbow
shimmy 'cross Alaska's sky
in a skirt of night and light.

Paper Candleholders

Next day, Grandma lays out paper bags,
scissors, and paint, teaching me
a kind of magic she and Mama used to make
every December, in New Mexico.

Luminarias
NEW MEXICO

I scalloped the tops,
Mom painted happy faces.
After we were done,
our brown bag candleholders
bloomed bright, lighting up the night.

Who Is She?

It's funny to think of Mama
making a mess with arts and crafts
or playing, sand in her hair,
giggling like a kid—like me!

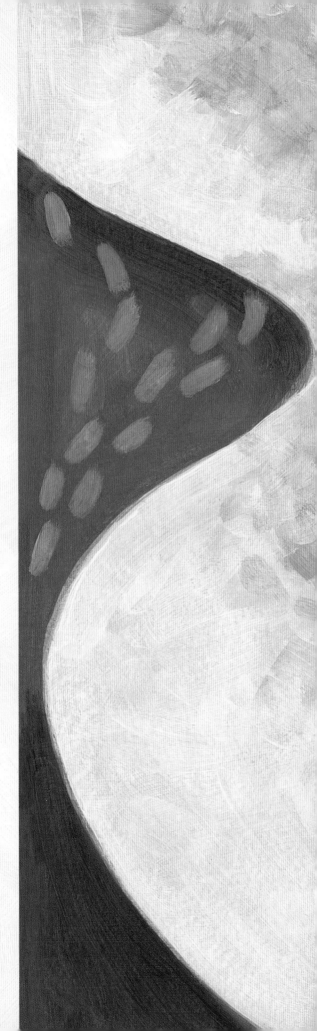

White Sands National Monument
NEW MEXICO

I scaled the first dune,
brother close behind. On three,
we rolled down the mound,
tumbling in sand and laughter,
ready to do it again.

Snow Dream

I flip through old photos of Mama,
smile at the snowman that stands
taller than she. I never get to see
snow where we live.

Colorado Springs
COLORADO

*Dad came home with skis
short as my little-girl legs.
I strapped them on tight,
shuffled across the backyard,
flying downhill—in my dreams.*

Imagine

Three days of not seeing my mama
feels like forever.
I bet she used to miss her dad,
gone for months.

Garden of the Gods
COLORADO

On Bring Your Dad Day,
I brought along a photo
of the two of us
at the Garden of the Gods.
I clutched my photo, wishing. . . .

Boys

Guys at school tease me
for collecting rocks "like a boy."
Next time, I'll tell them to
gather sharks' teeth "like a girl"!

Cherry Point
NORTH CAROLINA

Any day's perfect
for walking the river's edge.
I slipped over rocks,
gathered bruises and sharks' teeth
to show Dad when he's on leave.

Sailing

Pictures of kayaks and canoes
swim on the blue of our walls
thanks to Mama, who buys them all.
Now I think I know why.

Accotink Bay
VIRGINIA

The bay called us three.
We silently kayaked near
the bird-breeding box.
If only Dad would let us
clamber atop it and dance!

City Slicker

We've lived in the city
long as I can remember,
but Mama is always going on about
nature and the wonders of the woods.

Brackenridge Park
TEXAS

Dad says I'm lucky.
Mom sent me horseback riding
in the morning mist,
and as it cleared, I spotted
a great, green heron lift, soar!

Who Wears the Crown?

Grandma and I
watch *The Princess Bride*.
The story makes me
want to play Queen, like Mama.

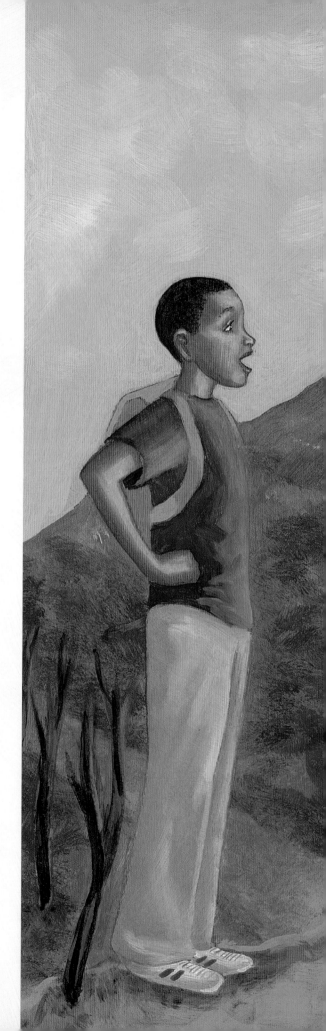

Gone Hiking
GERMANY

Saw my first castle
hiking in Hohenecken.
Queen of the hilltop,
I commanded my brother
to cease his laughing, and bow.

Chopsticks

At dinner I ask Grandma
for the chopsticks Mama
taught me to use. Once, I asked Mama
where she learned, and she just smiled.

Cherry Blossoms
JAPAN

Spring! Kimono time.
I joined the parade of girls
strolling avenues
dusted with cherry blossoms.
I caught a few, like snowflakes.

Tent

I set up a tent
in Grandma's backyard,
take a flashlight so I can read.
Mama's poems and me go camping.

Class Trip
JAPAN

My class camping trip!
Rhinoceros beetles and
dragonflies joined us.
We ate squid-on-a-stick, slept
at the foot of Mount Fuji.

Moving Day

I don't know how she did it,
moving all the time.
I get dizzy thinking about
all those good-byes.

Station Next
PORTUGAL

Move Number—who knows?
We call them all adventures.
I pack my poems,
wishing I could fold my friends
and slip them in my suitcase.

Endings

Grandma calls me to dinner,
but I read Mama's last poem
one more time.

Pride
WASHINGTON, DC, AREA

My heart dances when
Air Force One flings its shadow
across our front porch.
Dad promises we'll see this
countless times, because we're home.

Time to Go

Mama comes for me tomorrow.
I have a surprise for her.
I've been busy writing
poems of my own.

Let's See

Pencil and paper,
hole punch and ribbon—all set.
I work past bedtime,
copy Mama's poems, then
stitch them together with mine.

Back to the Attic

I put Mama's poems back in the chest
where I found them
and leave a stack of mine
for someone else to find.

The Gift

I run to Mama,
tackle her with hugs, kisses,
then hand her the book.
Breathlessly, I wait for her
to unwrap our memories.

AUTHOR'S NOTE

I moved around from home to home, and from city to city, when I was growing up, and I never had a choice in the matter. I remember what it felt like to change schools, and change addresses, without having any say. I would make friends in one place, have to leave them, then make friends in a new place, knowing one day I'd have to move on and say good-bye to them as well. That's also what life is like for military brats—children with a parent (or parents) serving in the armed forces.

I have a lot of friends who grew up as military brats, and I began to wonder how they made the most of a childhood spent in transition. In my own life, it was writing that helped me cope, and so I began to imagine a story about a military brat who also relied on writing to get her through.

Poems in the Attic is a work of fiction inspired by stories friends shared about growing up with parents who served in the United States military. In real life, service families might stay at one military base, or station, for two years or more. In my story, though, I wanted to cover a wide variety of locations where US military families serve, so my fictional family moves more frequently. However often military brats move, their stories remind me that, while we can't always choose our circumstances, we can choose how we respond to them. That's an important idea—for all of us.

UNITED STATES AIR FORCE BASES

Poems in the Attic is set in places around the United States and around the globe. Some poems are based on the recollections of people whose parents were in the US Army, while other poems reflect the memories of people whose moms or dads served in the Navy or the Air Force. For the purposes of my book, I had to choose one branch of the military for my character and her family, and I chose the Air Force.

Following is a list of Air Force bases in the states and countries where the poems are set. I am grateful for the men and women who continue to serve our country in these far-flung places, and I'm proud of the young people who learn to make the most of this life of constant change.

+ Los Angeles Air Force Base, El Segundo, California, USA ("Cabrillo Beach")
+ Joint Base Elmendorf-Richardson, Anchorage, Alaska, USA ("Aurora Borealis")
+ Holloman Air Force Base, Alamogordo, New Mexico, USA ("Luminarias," "White Sands National Monument")
+ Peterson Air Force Base, Colorado Springs, Colorado, USA ("Colorado Springs," "Garden of the Gods")
+ Seymour Johnson Air Force Base, Goldsboro, North Carolina, USA ("Cherry Point")
+ Joint Base Langley-Eustis, Hampton, Virginia, USA ("Accotink Bay")
+ Joint Base San Antonio/Lackland Air Force Base, San Antonio, Texas, USA ("Brackenridge Park")
+ Ramstein Air Base, Kaiserslautern, Germany ("Gone Hiking")
+ Yokota Air Base, Honshu, Japan ("Cherry Blossoms," "Class Trip")
+ Lajes Field, Terceira, Azores, Portugal ("Station Next")
+ Joint Base Andrews/Andrews Air Force Base, Camp Springs, Maryland, USA ("Pride")

POETRY FORMS

Poetry is my favorite form of storytelling, and in *Poems in the Attic* I used two forms of poetry: free verse and tanka. I wrote free verse poems for the parts of the story told by my present-day narrator and tanka poems for the parts told by her mother. At the very end of the book, though, both forms are used for our present-day narrator.

Free Verse

Free verse poems are lines of poetry that have no set rules. The lines can be long or short, with as many, or as few, syllables as the poet chooses. The poet sets his or her own rhythm and decides whether to use rhyme, repetition, metaphor, or some other element of poetry.

Free verse poetry can be the hardest of all forms because you have no set pattern to follow. You must make up your own rules as you go along, and those rules must make sense. No matter what rhythm or rhyme you create, the poem should look and sound like a poem when you're done. It seems easy, until you try it. But try it anyway!

Tanka

Tanka is an ancient poetry form, originally from Japan. The word tanka, as used here, means "short poem" in Japanese. The basic tanka is five lines long. The line-by-line syllable count varies in the modern English version, but the number of lines is always the same.

The modern form of tanka I chose to use for *Poems in the Attic* is as follows:

line 1: 5 syllables
line 2: 7 syllables
line 3: 5 syllables
line 4: 7 syllables
line 5: 7 syllables

Not every poet follows a syllable count for her or his tanka poems, but I think of a syllable count as a puzzle. Each word is a puzzle piece, and I like figuring out which words fit best.

Traditional tanka poems focus on mood. They are often about love, the four seasons, the shortness of life, or nature. In my tanka, I include mood, but in each poem my focus is more centered on telling a story.

I hope you have enjoyed the story I told, and I hope you'll try writing free verse and tanka poems of your own. Just think about telling a story or painting a picture using as few words as possible. You'll do fine! The main idea is to have fun with it. That's what poetry is all about.

The word is an
amazing thing.
Set it loose
upon a page,
let it blossom,
hear it sing!